Hello,

I hope that
you enjoy the
story. I hope
that it encourages
you to spend quality
time with your
loved ones.

Have a great day!

!! 2023

A Father's Love

Written by Alicia Smith

Illustrated by Olivia Smith H.

A Father's Love

Copyright 2022 by Alicia Smith

ISBN: 979-8-218-21299-5
Printed in the United States of America
Edited by: Naomi Books, LLC
Published by: literature4kids.org
Copyright 2022 by Alicia Smith

To my mother:

Thank you for always believing in me.

Thank you for your continued support, and thank you for your outpouring of love. You are my biggest fan, and for that, I am forever grateful.

With Love,

-Alicia

Thank you to my son, family and friends for believing in me.

-O.S.H

Rachelle happily asked, "Can we go on an adventure, Dad?"
Her dad, Will, said, "Yes. What would you like to do?"
"Can we ride our bikes to the park and play?"
"Yes, I like that idea."

Rachelle ran down the hallway. She went into
her bedroom and put on her shoes.
Then she ran outside to put her helmet on and get on her bike.
"Dad, I'm ready to go on the bike ride."
Dad said, "You know the way. Take the lead, and I will follow you."

When they arrived at the park,
Rachelle parked her bike and said,
"Dad, can we play our favorite game?"
"You like a lot of games," he said.
"Which game would you like to play?"

"Dad, you know I really
like to play Tag."
"Well then, I suggest
you run as fast as you
can before I tag you!"

Soon, Rachelle stopped and said, "I'm tired. Can we take a break from the game?"
"Yes. Would you like to play at the playground?"
Rachelle smiled and said, "Yes, I want to go on the swing. Can you push me, please?"
"Yes, I can. Thank you for asking nicely."

"Dad, can we take a ride to the ice cream shop?"
"Sure, ice cream sounds like a good idea.
But don't forget, you still need to get ready
for your school performance tonight."
"I understand, Dad," Rachelle said.

"Dad, what kind of ice cream are you having?"
"I'm not having ice cream today, but you can choose the flavor you want."
"Dad, can I have two scoops of the cherry ice cream?"
"Yes," Dad said. "But you can only eat one scoop now. We will save the rest for later."
"Thanks, Dad."

"Let's go home. You have a performance to get ready for."
They both got on their bikes and began riding down the street.
Rachelle said, "Dad, I feel scared
about the performance."
"Why are you scared? You have
practiced the dance for weeks."

"Yes, but I only practiced in front of my teacher, not in front of other people."
"I understand," said Dad. "I want you to do your best, have
fun, and be confident in yourself. You will do great."

Rachelle parked her bike, and then went to her bedroom. She put on her ballet clothes and shoes. Her dad walked down the hallway. He knocked on Rachelle's door. She said, "Come in, Dad."

He opened the door and said, "I will do your hair so you will look and feel beautiful." "Yes, Dad. I would like that."

When they arrived at the school, Rachelle sat in a chair next to her dad.
She leaned toward him and said, "I will show you my best ballet move."
Dad said, "I want to see them all."
Rachelle stood up, twirled around, and gave her dad a
hug. Then she walked away and joined her class.

The dancers happily walked onto the stage and began their performance. They did great!

At the end of their performance, the dance instructor said, "Thank you, everyone, for being courageous and working together as a team. I'm proud of you all for your hard work. Thank you to all the parents for helping your children during their ballet class."

When the students were dismissed, Rachelle ran
to her dad and said, "I felt scared, but I did it!"
"You looked like a superstar! Good job! I knew
you could do it," Dad said.
"Thank you, Dad."
He put his hand out and
gave Rachelle a high five.
"Let's go home," he said.

"Dad, can we have a dance party before I go to bed?"
"Yes, let's dance, but we will get ready for bed soon."
"Can we play for five more minutes, Dad?"
"Of course we can!"

"Rachelle, the dance party is over now. Can you choose a book you want to read?"
Rachelle found a book and her dad read the story out loud. At the end of the story, she said, "Dad, I had a fun day with you."
"I did too," said her dad.

"Goodnight, Rachelle. Sweet dreams."
"Goodnight, Dad."

About the Author

My name is Alicia Smith, I'm from California, and I'm an educator. I enjoy traveling, listening to various podcasts, and mentoring young children. I was inspired to become an author because of an experience I encountered with my students, which led me to create my first book, "The Mess." The story encourages children to be responsible and it incorporates a fun game of team work while cleaning their mess. Furthermore, I was inspired to write "A Father's love" because of my childhood interactions. The book focuses on having a positive role model, establishing healthy relationships, and highlights the importance of quality time with parents and loved ones. I enjoy writing books because I'm sharing positive messages that children can relate to. I also believe that children can learn valuable lessons and it's a great way for me to use my imagination. I hope you enjoyed the story. Thank you so much for your support!